Stray Birds

泰戈爾詩選 /

附
情境配樂
中英朗讀QR Code
＆紀念藏書票

漂鳥集

羅賓德拉納德・泰戈爾———著

Rabindranath Tagore

鄭振鐸———譯

笛藤出版

前 言

唯美詩化的文字，猶如夜幕蒼穹中的密佈星羅，自悠久的歷史長河之中散發出璀璨迷人的耀目光環，是人類精神世界中無價的瑰寶。千百年來，由各種文字所組成的篇章，經由傳遞淬煉，使其在各種文學彙集而成的花園中不斷綻放出絢幻之花，讓人們沈浸於美好的閱讀時光。

作者們以凝練的語言、鮮明的節奏，反映著世界萬象的生活樣貌，並以各種形式向世人展現他們內心豐富多彩的情感世界。每個民族、地域的文化都有其精妙之處，西洋文學往往直接抒發作者的思想，愛、自由、和平，言盡而意亦盡，毫無造作之感。

18~19 世紀，西洋文學的發展進入彰顯浪漫主義色彩的時期。所謂浪漫主義，就是用熱情奔放的言辭、絢麗多彩的想像與直陳誇張的表現手法，直接抒發出作者對理想世界熱切追求與渴望的情感。《世界經典文學 中英對照》系列，精選了浪漫主義時期一些作者們的代表作，包括泰戈爾的《新月集》、《漂鳥集》；雪萊的《西風頌》；濟慈的《夜鶯頌》；拜倫的《漫步在美的光影》；葉慈的《塵世玫瑰》。讓喜文之人盡情地徜徉於優美的字裡行間，領略作者及作品的無盡風采，享受藝術與美的洗禮。本系列所精選出的作品在世界文學領域中皆為經典名作，因此特別附上英文，方便讀者對照賞析英文詩意之美，並可同時提升英文閱讀與寫作素養。

在這一系列叢書當中，有對自然的禮讚，有對愛與和平的歌頌，有對孩童時代的讚美，也有對人生哲理的警示……，作者們在其一生中經歷了數次變革，以文字的形式寫下了無數天真、優美、現實、或悲哀的篇章，以無限的情懷吸引著所有各國藝文人士。文學界的名人郭沫若與冰心便是因受到了泰戈爾這位偉大的印度著名詩人所著詩歌的影響，在一段時期內寫出了許多類似的詩作。在世界文學界諸多名人當中有貴族、政治名人、社會名流、也有普羅大眾，他們來自不同的國家、種族，無論一生平順或是坎坷；但其所創作品無一不是充滿了對世間的熱愛，對未來美好世界的無限嚮往。

♪ 情境配樂 中·英朗讀 MP3

請掃描左方 QRcode 或輸入連結收聽：

https://bit.ly/poetstraybirds

◆ 英文配音：stephanie buckley
◆ 中文配音：陳余寬

漂鳥集。

Stray Birds

001

Stray birds of summer come to my window
to sing and fly away.
And yellow leaves of autumn, which have no songs,
flutter and fall there with a sigh.

夏天的漂鳥來到我窗前歌唱，又飛走了。
秋天的黃葉不唱歌，只輕嘆一聲，顫動飄落。

002

O troupe of little vagrants of the world,
leave your footprints in my words.

世界上的一群小流浪者呀，
請將你們的足跡留在我的字裡行間。

003

The world puts off its mask of vastness to its lover.
It becomes small as one song, as one kiss of the eternal.

面對著愛人，世界揭下了浩瀚的面具。
它變得小如一首歌，小如一個永恆的吻。

004

It is the tears of the earth that keep her smiles in bloom.

大地的眼淚，讓她永遠燦笑如花。

005

The mighty desert is burning for the love of a blade of
grass who shakes her head and laughs and flies away.

廣袤的沙漠熱烈地追求著一葉綠草的愛，
但她搖頭，微笑著，然後飛逝。

006

If you shed tears when you miss the sun,
you also miss the stars.

如果錯過太陽時你在流淚，
那麼你也會錯過繁星。

007

The sands in your way beg for your song and your
movement, dancing water.
Will you carry the burden of their lameness?

舞動的流水呀，沿途的泥沙向你乞求歌曲與樂章。
你願意承擔並帶著跛足的泥沙前行嗎？

008

Her wistful face haunts my dreams like the rain at night.

她熱切的臉龐，如夜雨般縈繞在我的夢境中。

009

Once we dreamt that we were strangers.
We wake up to find that we were dear to each other.

有一次，我們夢見彼此互不相識。
醒來時，才發現我們彼此親愛。

010

Sorrow is hushed into peace in my heart
like the evening among the silent trees.

憂傷在我的心中歸於平靜，
有如黃昏時身處寂靜的樹林裡。

011

Some unseen fingers, like idle breeze,
are playing upon my heart the music of the ripples.

有些看不見的手指，
像慵懶微風在我心上彈奏著篇篇樂章。

012

"What language is thine, O sea?"
"The language of eternal question."
"What language is thy answer, O sky?"
"The language of eternal silence."

「海水啊，你說的是什麼？」
「是永恆的疑問。」
「天空啊，你的答案是什麼？」
「是永恆的沉默。」

013

Listen, my heart, to the whispers of the world
with which it makes love to you.

聽啊，我的心，聆聽世界的低語，
這是它在對你示愛。

014

The mystery of creation is like the darkness of night
—it is great.
Delusions of knowledge are like the fog of the morning.

創造的奧秘如夜晚的黑暗般
—偉哉大哉。
而知識的妄想則如晨間之霧。

015

Do not seat your love upon a precipice because it is high.

不要因為懸崖高聳，就讓你的愛情高踞於上。

016

I sit at my window this morning where the world like a passer-by stops for a moment, nods to me and goes.

今晨我坐在窗前，
世界如一個路過的行人，
停留一會兒，
向我點點頭又走了。

017

These little thoughts are the rustle of leaves;
they have their whisper of joy in my mind.

這些微思是樹葉的颯颯聲；
在我心裡愉快地交頭接耳。

018

What you are you do not see,
what you see is your shadow.

你看不見自己的真面目，
你所見的，只是自己的影子。

My wishes are fools, they shout across thy songs,
my Master.
Let me but listen.

主呀，我的那些癡愚願望，竟摻雜在您的歌聲中嚷嚷著。
讓我只是靜靜聽著就好。

I cannot choose the best.
The best chooses me.

我無法選擇最好的事物。
是最好的事物選擇了我。

They throw their shadows before them who carry their
lantern on their back.

那些背燈者把影子投向自己面前。

That I exist is a perpetual surprise which is life.

我的存在，是一個永恆的驚喜，亦即生命。

023

"We, the rustling leaves, have a voice that answers the storms, but who are you so silent?"
"I am a mere flower."

「我們，是颯颯作響的樹葉，會發出聲響回應暴風雨，
　但沉默的你是誰呢？」
「我只是一朵花。」

024

Rest belongs to the work as the eyelids to the eyes.

休息之於工作，正如眼瞼之於眼睛。

025

Man is a born child, his power is the power of growth.

人類如同新生兒，他的力量即為成長的力量。

026

God expects answers for the flowers he sends us,
not for the sun and the earth.

上帝饋贈花束給我們，期待得到回應，
而祂贈予太陽與土地，則不求回報。

027

The light that plays, like a naked child, among the green
leaves happily knows not that man can lie.

光線宛若赤子在綠葉間愉快地嬉戲，
全然不知人間充滿虛偽欺瞞。

028

O beauty, find thyself in love,
not in the flattery of thy mirror.

美麗呀，在愛中尋找自我吧，不要只聽信諂媚的鏡子。

029

My heart beats her waves at the shore of the world and
writes upon it her signature in tears with the words, "I
love thee."

我的心將浪花打在世界之岸上，流著淚在岸上署名，
寫著：「我愛你。」

030

"Moon, for what do you wait?"
"To salute the sun for whom I must make way."

「月亮，你在等待什麼呢？」
「我要讓路給太陽，並向它致敬。」

031

The trees come up to my window
like the yearning voice of the dumb earth.

綠樹長到窗前，
彷彿瘖啞的大地發出渴望之聲。

032

His own mornings are new surprises to God.

對上帝而言，親手創造的清晨也充滿無限驚奇。

033

Life finds its wealth by the claims of the world,
and its worth by the claims of love.

生命因應世界的要求而得到財富，
因應愛的要求而得到價值。

034

The dry river-bed finds no thanks for its past.

乾枯的河床發覺無人對它的過去表示感謝。

035

The bird wishes it were a cloud.
The cloud wishes it were a bird.

鳥兒願為一朵雲。
雲兒願為一隻鳥。

036

The waterfall sings,
"I find my song, when I find my freedom."

瀑布唱著：「尋獲自由時，我就能唱出自己的歌了。」

037

I cannot tell why this heart languishes in silence.
It is for small needs it never asks, or knows or remembers.

我不明白這顆心為什麼默默頹喪著。
是為了它從不要求、不懂、或不記得的小小需求。

038

Woman, when you move about in your household service
your limbs sing like a hill stream among its pebbles.

婦人啊，當你在奔波整理家務時，你的手足就彷彿山間的
溪水流過小卵石般地歡樂吟唱著。

039

The sun goes to cross the Western sea,
leaving its last salutation to the East.

太陽橫跨過西方的海面時，
向東方獻上最後的致敬。

040

Do not blame your food because you have no appetite.

不要因為自己沒有胃口，而怪罪於食物。

041

The trees, like the longings of the earth,
stand a-tiptoe to peep at the heaven.

群樹如大地的渴望般聳立，窺看天空。

042

You smiled and talked to me of nothing
and I felt that for this I had been waiting long.

你微笑著，沒有對我說什麼話，
而我為此已等候許久。

043

The fish in the water is silent, the animal on the earth is
noisy, the bird in the air is singing.
But Man has in him the silence of the sea, the noise of the
earth and the music of the air.

水中的魚是沉靜的，陸地上的動物是喧鬧的，空中的飛鳥
會唱歌；但是人類卻兼容了海裡的沉靜，地上的喧鬧，與
天上的樂音。

044

The world rushes on over the strings of the lingering
heart making the music of sadness.

世界從躊躇的心弦上匆匆掠過，奏出悲傷的樂曲。

045

He has made his weapons his gods.
When his weapons win he is defeated himself.

他把武器奉為上帝。
當武器得勝，他卻輸給自己。

046

God finds himself by creating.

上帝從創造中找到自我。

047

Shadow, with her veil drawn, follows Light in secret meekness, with her silent steps of love.

「陰影」戴上她的面紗，以靜謐的愛之腳步，
默默地追隨著「光」。

048

The stars are not afraid to appear like fireflies.

繁星不怕自己顯得像螢火蟲。

049

I thank thee that I am none of the wheels of power but I am one with the living creatures that are crushed by it.

謝謝上帝，我不是權力之輪，
而是被壓在這輪下的活人之一。

050

The mind, sharp but not broad,
sticks at every point but does not move.

心是敏銳的，卻不寬廣。
它堅持己見不為所動。

051

Your idol is shattered in the dust to prove that God's dust is greater than your idol.

你的偶像消散於塵土中了，
證明上帝的塵土比你的偶像還偉大。

052

Man does not reveal himself in his history,
he struggles up through it.

人類無法於過往中展現自我，
唯有奮力掙扎嶄露頭角。

053

While the glass lamp rebukes the earthen for calling it cousin, the moon rises, and the glass lamp, with a bland smile, calls her, "My dear, dear sister."

玻璃燈責備瓦燈擅自稱他為表哥，
但是當月亮升起時，玻璃燈卻溫和地微笑著，
喚著「我親愛的，親愛的姊姊。」

054

Like the meeting of the seagulls and the waves we meet
and come near. The seagulls fly off, the waves roll away
and we depart.

如海鷗與波濤的相遇般,我們邂逅了、走近了。
海鷗飛散,波濤滾滾而逝,我們亦隨之別離。

055

My day is done, and I am like a boat drawn on the beach,
listening to the dance-music of the tide in the evening.

一日將盡,我像艘停泊於灘邊的小船,
靜靜聆聽著晚潮輕舞的樂聲。

056

Life is given to us, we earn it by giving it.

生命是上天賦予的,我們唯有獻出生命,才能得到它。

057

We come nearest to the great
when we are great in humility.

當我們極為謙卑時,
我們便趨近於偉大。

058

The sparrow is sorry for the peacock
at the burden of its tail.

麻雀對孔雀尾巴上的負擔感到可憐。

059

Never be afraid of the moments
—thus sings the voice of the everlasting.

絕對不要害怕剎那
—永恆之聲這樣地唱著。

060

The hurricane seeks the shortest road by the no-road,
and suddenly ends its search in the Nowhere.

颶風在絕路中尋找捷徑，卻又旋即停在絕境終止追尋。

061

Take my wine in my own cup, friend.
It loses its wreath of foam
when poured into that of others.

朋友，來喝我酒杯裡的酒吧。
若是把酒倒進別人的杯子裡，
一圈圈的泡沫就會隨之消散。

062

The Perfect decks itself in beauty
for the love of the Imperfect.

「完美」因愛慕「不完美」，把自己裝飾得更美。

063

God says to man,
"I heal you therefore I hurt, love you therefore punish."

　上帝對人說道：
「我為治癒你而傷害你，我因愛你而懲罰你。」

064

Thank the flame for its light, but do not forget the
lampholder standing in the shade with constancy of
patience.

感謝火焰帶來光明，但別忘卻那堅守在黑暗中的燈臺。

065

Tiny grass, your steps are small,
but you possess the earth under your tread.

小草呀，你的步伐雖小，但卻擁有腳下的大地。

066

The infant flower opens its bud and cries, "Dear World, please do not fade."

花兒綻放了它的蓓蕾，
喊道：「親愛的世界啊，請不要凋謝。」

067

God grows weary of great kingdoms,
but never of little flowers.

上帝對於偉大帝國會感到厭倦，
卻永不厭倦小小的花朵。

068

Wrong cannot afford defeat but Right can.

錯誤經不起失敗，但是真理卻不怕失敗。

069

"I give my whole water in joy," sings the waterfall, "though little of it is enough for the thirsty."

瀑布歌唱道：「雖然口渴的人只需一些水便足夠，但我滿懷喜悅地傾洩所有。」

070

Where is the fountain that throws up these flowers
in a ceaseless outbreak of ecstasy?

以湧流不絕的狂喜將花朵拋上天的泉源，
來自何處呢？

071

The woodcutter's axe begged for its handle from the tree.
The tree gave it.

樵夫的斧頭向樹木乞求斧柄。
樹便給了它。

072

In my solitude of heart I feel the sigh of this widowed
evening veiled with mist and rain.

伴著雨霧的孤寡黃昏，
我感受到心中寂寥的嘆息。

073

Chastity is a wealth that comes from abundance of love.

貞潔是豐盈的愛情所孕育而生的財富。

074

The mist, like love, plays upon the heart of the hills
and brings out surprises of beauty.

霧，宛如愛情，在山峰心間嬉戲，
變幻出令人驚嘆的美。

075

We read the world wrong and say that it deceives us.

我們錯讀世界，卻說它欺騙我們。

076

The poet wind is out over the sea and the forest
to seek his own voice.

詩人的風，吹過海洋和森林，
追尋自己的歌聲。

077

Every child comes with the message
that God is not yet discouraged of man.

每個孩子的誕生，
都帶來神對於人類尚未失望的訊息。

078

The grass seeks her crowd in the earth.
The tree seeks his solitude of the sky.

綠草向大地尋求同伴。
樹木向天空尋求孤寂。

079

Man barricades against himself.

人常自己築堤擋路。

080

Your voice, my friend, wanders in my heart, like the
muffled sound of the sea among these listening pines.

我的朋友，你的聲音飄蕩在我的心裡，
像海水的低吟之聲，繞繚在靜心聆聽的松林間。

081

What is this unseen flame of darkness
whose sparks are the stars?

以繁星為火花，
這看不見的黑暗之火，到底是什麼？

082

Let life be beautiful like summer flowers
and death like autumn leaves.

讓生命如夏花般絢爛，讓死亡如秋葉之靜美。

083

He who wants to do good knocks at the gate;
he who loves finds the gate open.

那想做好人的，在門外敲著門；那愛人的，看見門敞開著。

084

In death the many becomes one;
in life the one becomes many.
Religion will be one when God is dead.

死後，眾化為一；
生時，一化為眾。
上帝死亡之時，宗教終將合而為一。

085

The artist is the lover of Nature,
therefore he is her slave and her master.

藝術家是大自然的情人，
因此他是自然的奴隸，也是她的主人。

086

"How far are you from me, O Fruit?"
"I am hidden in your heart, O Flower."

「噢，果實呀，你離我有多遠呢？」
「噢，花兒呀，我藏在你心裡呢。」

087

This longing is for the one who is felt in the dark,
but not seen in the day.

這份渴望是為了那個在黑夜裡感覺得到，
在白天裡卻看不見的人。

088

"You are the big drop of dew under the lotus leaf,
I am the smaller one on its upper side,"
said the dewdrop to the lake.

　露珠對湖水說道：
「你是荷葉下的大露珠，我是荷葉上的小露珠。」。

089

The scabbard is content to be dull
when it protects the keenness of the sword.

刀鞘保護刀使其鋒利，自己則心甘情願變鈍。

090

In darkness the One appears as uniform;
in the light the One appears as manifold.

在黑暗中，「一」宛如一體；
在光亮中，「一」便宛如眾多。

091

The great earth makes herself hospitable
with the help of the grass.

在綠草的襯托下，大地顯得殷勤好客。

092

The birth and death of the leaves are the rapid whirls of
the eddy whose wider circles move slowly among stars.

樹葉的生與死如漩渦般急速旋轉，
而更廣大的漩渦在繁星間緩慢流轉著。

093

Power said to the world, "You are mine".
The world kept it prisoner on her throne.
Love said to the world, "I am thine."
The world gave it the freedom of her house.

權力告訴世界：「你是我的。」
世界便把權力囚禁在她的寶座下。
愛情對世界說：「我是你的。」
世界便讓愛情得以在她屋內自由來去。

094

The mist is like the earth's desire.
It hides the sun for whom she cries.

濃霧彷彿是大地的慾望。
它藏起了大地所哭求的太陽。

095

Be still, my heart, these great trees are prayers.

平靜些吧，我的心，這些大樹都是祈禱者呀。

096

The noise of the moment
scoffs at the music of the Eternal.

瞬間的喧囂，譏笑著永恆的音樂。

097

I think of other ages that floated upon the stream of
life and love and death and are forgotten, and I feel the
freedom of passing away.

當我想起在生命之流上浮沈的歲月，
當我想起那些被遺忘的愛與死亡，
我便感受到離開塵世帶來的自由。

098

The sadness of my soul is her bride's veil.
It waits to be lifted in the night.

我靈魂裡的憂傷猶如她的新娘面紗。
這面紗等著在夜裡被掀開。

099

Death's stamp gives value to the coin of life; making it
possible to buy with life what is truly precious.

死之印記讓生命之幣有所價值；
使其能用生命來換取那些真正的寶物。

100

The cloud stood humbly in a corner of the sky.
The morning crowned it with splendour.

白雲謙遜地站在天之一隅。
晨光為他鑲上了斑斕色彩。

101

The dust receives insult and in return offers her flowers.

塵土受到侮辱，卻以花朵回報。

102

Do not linger to gather flowers to keep them, but walk on,
for flowers will keep themselves blooming all your way.

向前走吧，莫駐足流連採擷花朵，
花朵自會伴你一路盛開芬芳。

103

Roots are the branches down in the earth.
Branches are roots in the air.

根是大地的樹枝。
樹枝是天空的根。

104

The music of the far-away summer flutters around the
Autumn seeking its former nest.

遠去的夏音在秋日振翅翱翔，尋覓舊巢。

105

Do not insult your friend
by lending him merits from your own pocket.

別從自己的口袋裡掏出功績借給朋友，
這對他而言是種侮辱。

106

The touch of the nameless days clings to my heart
like mosses round the old tree.

那段無名歲月裡的感觸，縈繞於心，
如同攀附於老樹上的苔蘚。

107

The echo mocks her origin to prove she is the original.

回聲嘲笑著她的原聲，想證明她才是原聲。

108

God is ashamed when the prosperous boasts of His special
favour.

飛黃騰達之人自誇獨得上帝恩寵，卻讓上帝感到羞愧。

109

I cast my own shadow upon my path,
because I have a lamp that has not been lighted.

我把影子投影到前方路上，只因我尚有盞未點亮的燈。

110

Man goes into the noisy crowd
to drown his own clamour of silence.

人們走進喧嘩的人海裡，
為的是想淹沒自己內心的沉默所發出的吶喊。

111

That which ends in exhaustion is death, but the perfect
ending is in the endless.

「死亡」終止於枯竭，但「圓滿」卻無窮無盡。

112

The sun has his simple robe of light. The clouds are
decked with gorgeousness.

太陽穿著樸素的光之罩袍，雲朵卻因此披上絢麗彩衣。

113

The hills are like shouts of children who raise their arms,
trying to catch stars.

山峰如孩子般呼喊，高高揮舞雙臂，
想摘下天上的星星。

114

The road is lonely in its crowd for it is not loved.

道路雖然人群熙攘卻不被人所愛，它是寂寞的。

115

The power that boasts of its mischiefs is laughed at by the yellow leaves that fall, and clouds that pass by.

權力誇耀自己的惡行；
卻被落地的黃葉與飄過的浮雲嘲笑。

116

The earth hums to me today in the sun, like a woman at her spinning, some ballad of the ancient time in a forgotten tongue.

今天大地在陽光下對我哼唱，宛如織布的婦人，
用著早已被遺忘的語言，吟唱古老的歌謠。

117

The grass-blade is worth of the great world where it grows.

綠草無愧於它所生長的偉大世界。

Dream is a wife who must talk.
Sleep is a husband who silently suffers.

夢是一位喋喋不休的妻子。
睡眠是一位默默忍受的丈夫。

The night kisses the fading day whispering to his ear, "I am death, your mother. I am to give you fresh birth."

　夜吻著逝去的白天，輕輕地在他耳邊低語：
「我是死亡，是你的母親。我將賜予你新的生命。」

I feel, thy beauty, dark night, like that of the loved woman when she has put out the lamp.

黑夜啊，我感受到你的美了，
你的美宛若一位可愛女人熄燈之際。

I carry in my world
that flourishes the worlds that have failed.

在我的世界裡，
延續著曾讓已逝世界繁榮的事物。

122

Dear friend, I feel the silence of your great thoughts of
many a deepening eventide on this beach when I listen to
these waves.

親愛的朋友啊，當我靜聽著海濤聲時，有好幾次在深沈的
黃昏暮色裡，能從海岸上感受到你偉大思想的靜默。

123

The bird thinks it is an act of kindness
to give the fish a lift in the air.

鳥兒以為助魚升空是一種仁慈的舉動。

124

"In the moon thou sendest thy love letters to me,"
said the night to the sun.
"I leave my answers in tears upon the grass."

黑夜對太陽說：「在月色中，你給了我情書。」
　　　　　　「綠草上的淚珠就是我的回答。」

125

The Great is a born child; when he dies he gives his great
childhood to the world.

「偉大」是個初生的孩子，
當他死去，他把美好的孩提時代留給世界。

126

Not hammer strokes, but dance of the water sings
the pebbles into perfection.

不是槌的敲打，而是水的載歌載舞，
才使鵝卵石臻於完美。

127

Bees sip honey from flowers
and hum their thanks when they leave.
The gaudy butterfly is sure
that the flowers owe thanks to him.

蜂兒從花中採蜜，離開時嗡嗡鳴謝。
浮誇的蝴蝶卻認為花兒應該向他致謝。

128

To be outspoken is easy
when you do not wait to speak the complete truth.

若你不願費時等待只為說出完整的事實，
直言不諱簡單得多。

129

Asks the Possible to the Impossible,
"Where is your dwelling place?"
"In the dreams of the impotent," comes the answer.

「可能」問「不可能」說：「你住在什麼地方呢？」
它回答道：「在無能者的夢境裡。」

130

If you shut your door to all errors truth will be shut out.

如果你不願犯錯，真理也會被你關在門外。

131

I hear some rustle of things behind my sadness of heart,
— I cannot see them.

在我憂傷的內心中，我聽到有些東西沙沙作響
—我看不見它們。

132

Leisure in its activity is work.
The stillness of the sea stirs in waves.

當「閒暇」活動時便是「工作」。
靜止的海水晃動時便成波濤。

133

The leaf becomes flower when it loves.
The flower becomes fruit when it worships.

樹葉戀愛時便成了花。
花崇拜時便成了果實。

134

The roots below the earth claim no rewards for making
the branches fruitful.

地下的樹根使樹枝結實纍纍，卻不求回報。

135

This rainy evening the wind is restless.
I look at the swaying branches and ponder over the
greatness of all things.

雨夜，風吹不歇。
我望著搖曳的樹枝，感嘆萬物的偉大。

136

Storm of midnight, like a giant child awakened in the
untimely dark, has begun to play and shout.

子夜的風雨，
如同巨嬰過早地在黑夜裡醒來，開始嬉戲喧鬧。

137

Thou raisest thy waves vainly to follow thy lover.
O sea, thou lonely bride of the storm.

噢，海啊，你是暴風雨留下的寂寞新娘，
只能徒然地掀起波濤追尋情人。

138

"I am ashamed of my emptiness,"
said the Word to the Work.
"I know how poor I am when I see you,"
said the Work to the Word.

文字對工作說道：「我對自己的空洞感到慚愧。」
工作對文字說道：「當我看見你時，我才知道自己有多貧
乏。」

139

Time is the wealth of change, but the clock in its parody
makes it mere change and no wealth.

時間是變化所擁有的財富，
但時鐘拙劣的模仿，
只帶來變化，卻沒有財富。

140

Truth in her dress finds facts too tight.
In fiction she moves with ease.

「真理」著裝後，覺得「事實」太束縛了，
在「虛構」中，她才能活動自如。

141

When I travelled to here and to there, I was tired of thee,
O Road, but now when thou leadest me to everywhere I am
wedded to thee in love.

當我四處漂浪時，路啊，我曾對你感到厭倦；而現在，無
論你引領我前往何處，我已在愛中與你合而為一。

142

Let me think that there is one among those stars
that guides my life through the dark unknown.

就讓我想像，繁星中，
會有一顆星指引著我的生命，走過未知的黑暗。

143

Woman, with the grace of your fingers you touched my
things and order came out like music.

女人，當你用優雅的手指碰觸我的一切，
宇宙秩序便如音樂般暢流湧現了。

144

One sad voice has its nest among the ruins of the years.
It sings to me in the night,—"I loved you."

一個憂傷的聲音，棲息在歲月的廢墟中。
它在夜裡對我唱著—「我曾深愛過你。」

145

The flaming fire warns me off by its own glow.
Save me from the dying embers hidden under ashes.

燃燒的火燄散發著灼光禁止我靠近。
請將我從埋藏在灰中的餘燼裡救出來吧。

146

I have my stars in the sky,
But oh for my little lamp unlit in my house.

滿天繁星為我所有，
但我卻為我屋裡的小燈沒有點亮而嘆息。

147

The dust of the dead words clings to thee.
Wash thy soul with silence.

已逝之語化為塵土沾附於你。
用沉默洗淨你的靈魂吧。

148

Gaps are left in life
through which comes the sad music of death.

生命留下許多縫隙，
隙間傳出陣陣死之哀歌。

149

The world has opened its heart of light in the morning.
Come out, my heart, with thy love to meet it.

世界在早晨敞開了它的光明之心。
出來吧，我的心，帶著愛去與它相會。

150

My thoughts shimmer with these shimmering leaves and
my heart sings with the touch of this sunlight; my life is
glad to be floating with all things into the blue of space,
into the dark of time.

我的思緒，隨著這些閃耀的綠葉而閃耀著，
我的心靈，受到日光拂照也唱起歌來；
我的生命，隨萬物徜徉在空間的蔚藍與時間的暗黑中，
感到愉悅。

151

God's great power is in the gentle breeze, not in the storm.

上帝顯能於輕柔的微風中，而非狂風暴雨裡。

152

This is a dream in which things are all loose and they oppress. I shall find them gathered in thee when I awake and shall be free.

在夢中，萬物崩解且壓迫著我。
醒來時，我會發現萬物歸聚於您，我也將得以自由。

153

"Who is there to take up my duties?"
asked the setting sun.
"I shall do what I can, my Master,"
said the earthen lamp.

落日問道：「有誰要接替我的工作呢？」
瓦燈答道：「我會盡我所能，我的主人。」

154

By plucking her petals
you do not gather the beauty of the flower.

摘下花瓣，無法得到花的美。

163

"The learned say that your lights will one day be no
more," said the firefly to the stars.
The stars made no answer.

螢火蟲對天上的星星道：
「學者說，你的光總有一天會消失的。」
天上的星星不回答它。

164

In the dusk of the evening the bird of some early dawn
comes to the nest of my silence.

在黃昏的微光裡，晨鳥來到了我靜謐的巢中。

165

Thoughts pass in my mind like flocks of ducks in the sky.
I hear the voice of their wings.

思緒掠過我心，如一群野鴨飛過天際。
我聽見牠們的振翅之聲了。

166

The canal loves to think
that rivers exist solely to supply it with water.

運河總喜歡想：河流的存在，是專為它而供水的。

167

The world has kissed my soul with its pain, asking for its return in songs.

世界用它的痛苦親吻我的靈魂，要求以歌聲作為回報。

168

That which oppresses me, is it my soul trying to come out in the open, or the soul of the world knocking at my heart for its entrance?

壓迫著我的，究竟是我那想要掙脫而出的靈魂，
抑或是世界的靈魂，敲著我的心門想要進來呢？

169

Thought feeds itself with its own words and grows.

思想以他獨有的言語餵養自己，得以成長茁壯。

170

I have dipped the vessel of my heart into this silent hour; it has filled with love.

我把心之容器輕輕浸入靜謐時刻，
讓它充滿愛。

171

Either you have work or you have not.
When you have to say, "Let us do something,"
then begins mischief.

不論你有工作，或者沒有。
當你不得不說：「讓我們做些事吧。」
那麼麻煩就來了。

172

The sunflower blushed to own the nameless flower as her kin.
The sun rose and smiled on it, saying, "Are you well, my darling?"

向日葵羞於把無名小花看作她的同類。
太陽升上來了，向小花微笑，說道：「你好嗎，親愛的？」。

173

"Who drives me forward like fate?"
"The Myself striding on my back."

「誰像命運般地將我驅策向前？」
「那是我自己，在背後闊步前行。」

174

The clouds fill the watercups of the river,
hiding themselves in the distant hills.

雲把水倒進河的水杯裡，自己隱身在遠山之中。

175

I spill water from my water jar as I walk on my way.
Very little remains for my home.

我一路走著，水不斷從水瓶裡灑出來。
只留下極少的水可供家裡使用。

176

The water in a vessel is sparkling;
the water in the sea is dark.
The small truth has words that are clear;
the great truth has great silence.

容器中的水閃閃發光；
而海裡的水暗黑沉沉。
微小的真理可以用文字話語闡述清楚；
偉大的真理卻深邃沉默。

177

Your smile was the flowers of your own fields, your talk
was the rustle of your own mountain pines, but your heart
was the woman that we all know.

你的微笑，是你自己田園裡的花朵，
你的談吐，是你自己山中的松濤，
但是你的心呀，卻似那個我們全都熟悉的女人。

178

It is the little things that I leave behind for my loved
ones,—great things are for everyone.

偉大事物歸於眾人，但小禮物留給我珍愛的人。

179

Woman, thou hast encircled the world's heart with the
depth of thy tears as the sea has the earth.

女人啊，你用深邃的眼淚包圍著世界之心，
有如大海圍繞著大地。

180

The sunshine greets me with a smile.
The rain, his sad sister, talks to my heart.

太陽以微笑向我問候。
而雨水，他那憂傷的姊姊，與我談心。

181

My flower of the day dropped its petals forgotten.
In the evening it ripens into a golden fruit of memory.

我的白晝之花，落下它那被遺忘的花瓣。
黃昏時分，花朵長成一顆記憶的金果。

182

I am like the road in the night
listening to the footfalls of its memories in silence.

我像那夜間之路，
正靜悄悄地聽著記憶的足音。

183

The evening sky to me is like a window, and a lighted
lamp, and a waiting behind it.

黃昏的天空，在我看來像一扇窗戶、一盞燈火，
以及燈火背後的等待。

184

He who is too busy doing good finds no time to be good.

太忙於做好事的人，反而找不到時間修養自己。

185

I am the autumn cloud, empty of rain,
see my fullness in the field of ripened rice.

我是秋天的雲朵，空空地不帶著雨水，
但在成熟的稻田中，看見了我的豐美。

186

They hated and killed and men praised them.
But God in shame hastens to hide its memory
under the green grass.

他們彼此仇恨殘殺，人類反而稱讚他們。
然而上帝感到羞愧，急忙地把記憶埋藏在綠草之下。

187

Toes are the fingers that have forsaken their past.

腳趾乃是捨棄了過去的手指。

188

Darkness travels towards light,
but blindness towards death.

黑暗往光明處前行，
而盲目卻走向死亡。

189

The pet dog suspects the universe
for scheming to take its place.

受寵的小狗懷疑宇宙密謀篡奪牠的地位。

190

Sit still my heart, do not raise your dust.
Let the world find its way to you.

靜靜坐著吧，我的心，不要揚起你的塵土。
讓世界自己找到你。

191

The bow whispers to the arrow before it speeds forth,
—"Your freedom is mine."

弓在箭要射出之前，低聲對箭說道：
—「你的自由是屬於我的。」

192

Woman, in your laughter
you have the music of the fountain of life.

女人啊，你的笑聲裡流淌著生命之泉的樂音。

193

A mind all logic is like a knife all blade.
It makes the hand bleed that uses it.

只有理智的心，有如一把全是鋒刃的刀。
會讓持刀的手流血。

194

God loves man's lamp lights
better than his own great stars.

上帝愛人間的燈火，更勝於他自己的偉大星辰。

195

This world is the world ot wild storms
kept tame with the music of beauty.

這世界的狂風暴雨，都被美之樂音所馴服了。

196

"My heart is like the golden casket of thy kiss,"
said the sunset cloud to the sun.

落日時分的雲彩向太陽說：
「我的心就像金色的首飾盒，裝著你的吻。」

197

By touching you may kill,
by keeping away you may possess.

碰觸我，你或許會被殺害，遠離我，你或許能夠擁有。

198

The cricket's chirp and the patter of rain come to me
through the dark, like the rustle of dreams from my past
youth.

蟋蟀的唧唧，夜雨的淅瀝，穿過黑暗傳到我耳邊，
好似我已逝的少年時代，窸窣地來到我的夢境。

199

"I have lost my dewdrop," cries the flower to the morning
sky that has lost all its stars.

黎明的天空失去了所有的星辰，
花兒對他喊著：「我的露珠不見了。」

200

The burning log bursts in flame and cries,
—"This is my flower, my death."

燃燒著的木塊，冒出火花並喊著，
—「這是我的花朵，我的死亡。」

201

The wasp thinks that the honey-hive
of the neighbouring bees is too small.
His neighbours ask him to build one still smaller.

黃蜂認為隔鄰蜜蜂用來儲蜜的蜂巢太小。
但鄰居卻要求他去蓋一個更小的蜂巢。

202

"I cannot keep your waves," says the bank to the river.
"Let me keep your footprints in my heart."

河岸向河流說：「我留不住你的波浪。」
「讓我把你的足跡深印在我的心裡吧。」

203

The day, with the noise of this little earth,
drowns the silence of all worlds.

白晝，藉由這小小地球上的喧囂，
淹沒了整個宇宙的寂靜。

204

The song feels the infinite in the air, the picture in the
earth, the poem in the air and the earth;
For its words have meaning that walks
and music that soars.

歌聲在空中感到無限，圖畫在地上感到無限，
詩呢，無論在空中、在地上都是如此；
因為詩的文字含有能行走的意義與能飛翔的音韻。

205

When the sun goes down to the West, the East of his
morning stands before him in silence.

當太陽在西方落下時，
他在東方的早晨已靜悄悄地站在面前。

206

Let me not put myself wrongly to my world and set it
against me.

讓我在自己的世界裡不會有錯誤的定位，
也不會自我抵抗。

207

Praise shames me, for I secretly beg for it.

榮譽羞辱著我，因為我暗地裡向它乞求。

208

Let my doing nothing when I have nothing to do become
untroubled in its depth of peace like the evening in the
seashore when the water is silent.

當我無事可做時，就讓我什麼都不做，
不受干擾地陷入安靜吧，
一如平靜無波時的海邊暮色。

209

Maiden, your simplicity, like the blueness of the lake,
reveals your depth of truth.

少女啊，你的單純如湖水般蔚藍，
顯露出你的真摯深切。

210

The best does not come alone.
It comes with the company of the all.

最好的事物不會獨自前來。
它會伴隨所有的事物同來。

211

God's right hand is gentle, but terrible is his left hand.

上帝的右手是慈愛的，但是祂的左手卻令人敬畏。

212

My evening came among the alien trees and spoke in a
language which my morning stars did not.

暮色從陌生的林間走來，
訴說著晨星聽不懂的話語。

213

Night's darkness is a bag
that bursts with the gold of the dawn.

夜晚的黑暗像個袋子，突然綻放出金色曙光。

214

Our desire lends the colours of the rainbow
to the mere mists and vapours of life.

我們的慾望把彩虹的顏色，
借給那只不過是雲霧水氣般的人生。

215

God waits to win back his own flowers
as gifts from man's hands.

上帝等著要從人類的手上，
贏回他自己的花朵作為禮物。

216

My sad thoughts tease me asking me their own names.

我的憂思嘲笑我，問我它們的名字。

217

The service of the fruit is precious, the service of the flower is sweet, but let my service be the service of the leaves in its shade of humble devotion.

果實的奉獻是珍貴的，花朵的奉獻是甜美的，
但是讓我像綠葉般效勞，謙遜地奉獻一方樹蔭。

218

My heart has spread its sails to the idle winds for the shadowy island of Anywhere.

我的心乘著徐徐的風，揚起了帆，
隨風航向一處夢幻島。

219

Men are cruel, but Man is kind.

眾人是殘忍的，但個人是善良的。

220

Make me thy cup and let my fullness be for thee and for thine.

把我當做您的杯子，讓我為了您和您的一切而完滿。

221

The storm is like the cry of some god in pain
whose love the earth refuses.

狂風怒號著，有如求愛被大地拒絕的神祇般痛苦不堪。

222

The world does not leak because death is not a crack.

世界不會流失，因為死亡並不是一道裂縫。

223

Life has become richer by the love that has been lost.

生命因失去的愛情，而更為豐富。

224

My friend, your great heart shone with the sunrise of the East like the snowy summit of a lonely hill in the dawn.

我的朋友，你崇高的心閃耀著東方旭日的光芒，
正如黎明一座積雪的孤峰。

225

The fountain of death makes the still water of life play.

死亡的流泉，讓靜止的生命之水跳躍。

226

Those who have everything but thee, my God,
laugh at those who have nothing but thyself.

那些除了您以外擁有一切的人，我的上帝，
在嘲笑著一無所有但擁有您的人。

227

The movement of life has its rest in its own music.

生命的進行曲，隨著自己的曲調、休止、暫歇。

228

Kicks only raise dust and not crops from the earth.

頓足只會揚起塵土，卻無法從大地收成。

229

Our names are the light that glows on the sea waves at
night and then dies without leaving its signature.

我們的名字，如幽微的夜浪波光，
匆匆消逝，來不及留下印記。

230

Let him only see the thorns who has eyes to see the rose.

讓眼中只看得到玫瑰花的人，也好好定睛看看它的刺。

231

Set bird's wings with gold
and it will never again soar in the sky.

為鳥翼繫上黃金，這鳥兒便永遠不能在空中翱翔了。

232

The same lotus of our clime blooms here in the alien
water with the same sweetness, under another name.

我們地區的荷花在這陌生的水域裡綻放，
芳香依舊，只是名字改變了。

233

In heart's perspective the distance looms large.

從心出發，相隔的距離似乎更遠。

234

The moon has her light all over the sky,
her dark spots to herself.

月亮讓她的光芒遍照天際，卻自己獨留污痕。

235

Do not say, "It is morning," and dismiss it with a name of yesterday. See it for the first time as a new-born child that has no name.

不要因為「現在是早晨了」，就把它當成昨天的名詞予以捨棄。把它視為第一次見到的、還沒有名字的新生兒吧。

236

Smoke boasts to the sky, and Ashes to the earth,
that they are brothers to the fire.

炊煙對天空誇口，灰燼對大地吹噓，都說自己是火的兄弟。

237

The raindrop whispered to the jasmine,
"Keep me in your heart for ever."
The jasmine sighed, "Alas," and dropped to the ground.

雨點向茉莉花耳語：「把我永遠地留在你心裡吧。」
茉莉花嘆了口氣，「唉」，便輕落於地。

238

Timid thoughts, do not be afraid of me.
I am a poet.

膽怯的思想呀，不要怕我。
我是一個詩人。

239

The dim silence of my mind seems filled with crickets'
chirp — the grey twilight of sound.

我的心在朦朧的沉默裡，似乎充滿了蟋蟀的鳴聲—
那灰暮微亮的歌聲。

240

Rockets, your insult to the stars follows yourself back to
the earth.

火箭呀，你對於群星的侮辱，
又跟著你自己回到地面上來了。

241

Thou hast led me through my crowded travels of the day
to my evening's loneliness.
I wait for its meaning through the stillness of the night.

您曾經帶領著我，越過擁擠的白晝，
到達了我黃昏的孤寂之境。
在夜裡的靜謐中，我等待著它的意義。

242

This life is the crossing of a sea,
where we meet in the same narrow ship.
In death we reach the shore
and go to our different worlds.

此生，猶如橫渡大海時，我們在同一艘小船裡相聚。
死後，我們抵達岸邊，將往各自的世界去。

243

The stream of truth flows through
its channels of mistakes.

真理之川會流經它的錯誤之渠。

244

My heart is homesick today
for the one sweet hour across the sea of time.

我的心今天想家了，想著那跨過時間之海的甜蜜時刻。

245

The bird-song is the echo of
the morning light back from the earth.

鳥兒的歌聲是曙光碰觸大地後的回音。

246

"Are you too proud to kiss me?"
the morning light asks the buttercup.

晨光問毛茛說：「你太驕傲了，所以不願意吻我嗎？」

247

"How may I sing to thee and worship, O Sun?"
asked the little flower.
"By the simple silence of thy purity," answered the sun.

小花問道：「太陽呀，我要怎樣唱歌給你聽，
　　　　　　怎樣崇敬你呢？」
太陽答道：「我只要你簡單、安寧的純潔」。

248

Man is worse than an animal when he is an animal.

把人類看成野獸時，他比野獸還要壞。

249

Dark clouds become heaven's flowers
when kissed by light.

烏雲接受光芒之吻後，便成為天上的花朵。

250

Let not the sword-blade mock its handle for being blunt.

不要讓刀鋒譏笑刀柄的駑鈍。

251

The night's silence, like a deep lamp, is burning with the light of its milky way.

夜的靜謐，如燈盞久燃著銀河之光。

252

Around the sunny island of Life swells day and night death's limitless song of the sea.

在充滿陽光的生命之島上，
死亡如大海般無垠的歌聲，
日以繼夜地縈繞著。

253

Is not this mountain like a flower,
with its petals of hills, drinking the sunlight?

花瓣似的山峰飲著日光，
這座山不就像一朵花嗎？

254

The real with its meaning read wrong
and emphasis misplaced is the unreal.

當「真實」的含義被誤解，
輕重被倒置，就成了「不真實」。

255

Find your beauty, my heart, from the world's movement,
like the boat that has the grace of the wind and the water.

我的心呀，從世界的流動中，找尋你的美吧，
正如那小船得到風與水的優雅似的。

256

The eyes are not proud of their sight
but of their eyeglasses.

雙眼不以視力為傲，卻以戴著眼鏡為傲。

257

I live in this little world of mine and am afraid to make it
the least less. Lift me into thy world and let me have the
freedom gladly to lose my all.

我住在自己的小小世界裡，深怕它會再縮小一丁點兒。
讓我去到您的世界裡，自由自在開懷地捨棄我的所有。

258

The false can never grow into truth
by growing in power.

憑藉權力生長的虛偽，
永遠不會變成真實。

259

My heart, with its lapping waves of song,
longs to caress this green world of the sunny day.

我的心，跟著層疊的波浪歌唱著，
渴望著要撫摸晴朗的綠色世界。

260

Wayside grass, love the star,
then your dreams will come out in flowers.

路旁的小草，愛那天上的星辰吧，
那麼你的夢想便會在花朵裡實現了。

261

Let your music, like a sword,
pierce the noise of the market to its heart.

讓你的音樂如一柄利刃，
直刺市井喧擾的心中吧。

262

The trembling leaves of this tree touch my heart
like the fingers of an infant child.

這棵樹顫動的葉子，
就像嬰孩的手指，觸動著我的心。

263

The little flower lies in the dust.
It sought the path of the butterfly.

小花睡在塵土裡。
尋找蝴蝶走的路。

264

I am in the world of the roads. The night comes.
Open thy gate, thou world of the home.

我身處道路縱橫的世界中。
夜來了。打開您的門吧，家之世界。

265

I have sung the songs of thy day. In the evening let me
carry thy lamp through the stormy path.

我已經唱過了白天的歌。
在黃昏時分，讓我拿著燈走過風雨飄搖的道路吧。

266

I do not ask thee into the house.
Come into my infinite loneliness, my Lover.

我不請求你進到我的屋裡。
請走進我無邊無際的孤獨裡吧，我的愛人。

267

Death belongs to life as birth does. The walk is in the
raising of the foot as in the laying of it down.

死亡隸屬於生命，正如出生一樣。
邁開步伐是在走路，正如停下腳步也是在走路。

268

I have learnt the simple meaning of thy whispers in
flowers and sunshine—teach me to know thy words in pain
and death.

我已經學會了你在花與陽光裡微語的意義。
—再教我明白您所謂的痛苦與死亡。

269

The night's flower was late when the morning kissed her,
she shivered and sighed and dropped to the ground.

夜的花朵來晚了，當早晨吻著她時，
她顫慄著，嘆了口氣，落在地上了。

270

Through the sadness of all things
I hear the crooning of the Eternal Mother.

從萬物的愁苦中，我聽見了「永恆母親」的呻吟。

271

I came to your shore as a stranger, I lived in your house as
a guest, I leave your door as a friend, my earth.

我的大地啊，我到你岸上時是一個陌生人，住在你屋內時
是一個客人，離開你的門時是一個朋友。

272

Let my thoughts come to you, when I am gone, like the
after glow of sunset at the margin of starry silence.

當我走時，讓我的思緒到你那裡去，
如夕陽餘暉照耀在寂靜的星空邊際。

273

Light in my heart the evening star of rest
and then let the night whisper to me of love.

在我的心頭點亮那寧靜的暮星吧，
然後讓黑夜向我微語著愛情。

274

I am a child in the dark.
I stretch my hands through the coverlet of night for thee,
Mother.

我是一個在黑暗中的孩子。
從夜的被單裡向你伸出雙手，母親。

275

The day of work is done.
Hide my face in your arms, Mother.
Let me dream.

白天的工作結束了。讓我把臉藏在您的臂彎中，母親。
讓我入夢吧。

276

The lamp of meeting burns long;
it goes out in a moment at the parting.

相聚時刻，燈火長燃不滅；分離之際，轉瞬熄滅。

277

One word keep for me in thy silence, O World, when I am
dead, "I have loved."

世界啊，當我死去時，
請在沉默中替我留下「我曾愛過」這句話。

278

We live in this world when we love it.

我們熱愛世界時，才算是真正活在這世界上。

279

Let the dead have the immortality of fame,
but the living the immortality of love.

讓死者有不朽的名聲，但讓生者有不朽的愛。

280

I have seen thee as the half-awakened child sees his
mother in the dusk of the dawn and then smiles and sleeps
again.

我曾看見您，像半醒的嬰孩，在黎明的微光裡看見母親，
隨後微笑著又睡著了。

281

I shall die again and again
to know that life is inexhaustible.

我將死了又死，才能明白生命之無窮無盡。

282

While I was passing with the crowd in the road I saw thy smile from the balcony and I sang and forgot all noise.

當我和擁擠的人群一起走在路上時，我看見您從陽臺上送過來的微笑，我歌唱著，忘了所有的喧嘩。

283

Love is life in its fulness like the cup with its wine.

愛就是完整的生命，正如斟滿了酒的酒杯。

284

They light their own lamps and sing their own words
in their temples.
But the birds sing thy name in thine own morning light,
— for thy name is joy.

他們點亮自己的燈，在寺院裡喃喃吟唱自己的話語。
但是小鳥卻在您的晨光中，唱著您的名字
—因為您的名字便是快樂。

285

Lead me in the centre of thy silence
to fill my heart with songs.

帶領我到您沉靜的中心，讓我的心充滿歌聲吧。

286

Let them live who choose in their own hissing world of
fireworks.
My heart longs for thy stars, my God.

讓選擇了焰火嘶嘶的世界的那些人，生活在那裡吧。
我的心渴望著繁星，我的上帝。

287

Love's pain sang round my life like the unplumbed sea,
and love's joy sang like birds in its flowering groves.

愛的痛苦環繞著我的一生，像洶湧的大海般歌唱著，
而愛的快樂卻像鳥兒們在花叢中歌唱。

288

Put out the lamp when thou wishest.
I shall know thy darkness and shall love it.

假如您願意，就熄了燈吧。
我將明白您的黑暗，也將愛著它。

289

When I stand before thee at the day's end
thou shalt see my scars
and know that I had my wounds and also my healing.

當我在一日將盡之際站在您面前，您將看見我的傷疤，
明白我有過許多創傷和療癒。

290

Some day I shall sing to thee in the sunrise of some other
world, "I have seen thee before in the light of the earth, in
the love of man."

總有一天，我要在另一個世界的日出時對您唱道：「從前
我在地球的光裡，在人類的愛裡，已經見過您了。」

291

Clouds come floating into my life from other days
no longer to shed rain or usher storm
but to give colour to my sunset sky.

幾天前飄進我生命裡的烏雲，
請別再落下雨點或引起風暴了，
只要為我的夕陽染上色彩。

292

Truth raises against itself the storm
that scatters its seeds broadcast.

真理引起暴風雨，
風暴四處散播真理的種子。

293

The storm of the last night has crowned this morning
with golden peace.

昨夜的風雨讓今天早晨冠上了金色的和平。

294

Truth seems to come with its final word; and the final
word gives birth to its next.

真理似乎隨著最後的話語而出現，
而這最後的話語又產生了下一個真理。

295

Blessed is he whose fame does not outshine his truth.

他是受到祝福的，因為他的名聲並不會蓋過真實的內在。

296

Sweetness of thy name fills my heart when I forget
mine—like thy morning sun when the mist is melted.

當我忘卻自己姓名時，您甜美的名字充滿我心，
—如同旭日初升時，薄霧便消散。

297

The silent night has the beauty of the mother
and the clamorous day of the child.

靜謐的黑夜擁有母親之美，
而喧囂的白天則有孩童之美。

298

The world loved man when he smiled.
The world became afraid of him when he laughed.

當人類微笑時，世界愛著他。
但當他大笑時，世界便害怕了。

299

God waits for man to regain his childhood in wisdom.

上帝等著人類從智慧中重新獲得童年。

300

Let me feel this world as thy love taking form,
then my love will help it.

讓我感受世界，如同感受您的愛，
那麼，我的愛也將幫助它。

301

Thy sunshine smiles upon the winter days of my heart,
never doubting of its spring flowers.

您的陽光對著我心裡的冬天微笑著，
從來不懷疑它也有春天的花朵。

302

God kisses the finite in his love
and man the infinite.

上帝在他的愛裡吻著「有限」，
而人卻吻著「無限」。

303

Thou crossest desert lands of barren years
to reach the moment of fulfilment.

您橫越過荒蕪年歲的沙漠，
終而抵達了圓滿的時刻。

304

God's silence ripens man's thoughts into speech.

上帝的沉默，使人的思想成熟為語言。

305

Thou wilt find, Eternal Traveller,
marks of thy footsteps across my songs.

永恆的旅人呀，你可以在我的歌中找到你的足跡。

306

Let me not shame thee, Father,
who displayest thy glory in thy children.

我不會讓您丟臉的，父親，
您孩子們的身上顯現出您的榮光。

307

Cheerless is the day, the light under frowning clouds
is like a punished child with traces of tears on its pale
cheeks, and the cry of the wind is like the cry of a
wounded world. But I know I am travelling to meet my
Friend.

這一天並不愉快，卷雲下的光線有如受罰的孩童，蒼白的
臉頰上淚痕未乾，怒號的風有如受傷的世界在哭泣。
但我深知，自己正在旅行，要與朋友相見。

308

To night there is a stir among the palm leaves, a swell in
the sea, Full Moon, like the heart throb of the world.
From what unknown sky hast thou carried in thy silence
the aching secret of love?

今晚棕櫚葉在沙沙地作響,海潮洶湧。
滿月,有如世界的心跳。
帶著愛情痛苦的祕密,你在哪裡的天空沉默著?

309

I dream of a star, an island of light, where I shall be born
and in the depth of its quickening leisure my life will
ripen its works like the ricefield in the autumn sun.

我夢見了一顆星,一座光明之島,我將在那裡誕生,
在它的輕快悠閒中,我的生命將成熟如秋陽下的稻田。

310

The smell of the wet earth in the rain rises
like a great chant of praise
from the voiceless multitude of the insignificant.

雨中溼潤的土地氣息,就像從渺小默默的人群那裡,
傳來崇敬的讚美歌聲。

311

That love can ever lose
is a fact that we cannot accept as truth.

我們無法接受「愛情終將失去」的事實。

312

We shall know some day that death can never rob us of
that which our soul has gained, for her gains are one with
herself.

有一天我們將會明白，死亡永遠無法奪去靈魂所獲之物，
因為靈魂所獲得的，和她自己合為一體。

313

God comes to me in the dusk of my evening with the
flowers from my past kept fresh in his basket.

上帝在暮色微光中，帶著我過去的花朵前來，
在他的花籃中，這些花還依舊鮮活。

314

When all the strings of my life will be tuned, my Master,
then at every touch of thine will come out the music of
love.

主啊，當我的生命之弦都已調音時，
你的每一次彈奏，都可以演奏出愛的樂聲。

315

Let me live truly, my Lord,
so that death to me becomes true.

讓我真真實實地活著吧，我的上帝，
如此一來，死亡對我而言也會成為真實。

316

Man's history is waiting in patience for the triumph of
the insulted man.

人類的歷史，耐心等待著受辱者獲勝。

317

I feel thy gaze upon my heart this moment like the
sunny silence of the morning upon the lonely field whose
harvest is over.

這一刻我感受到你的目光正落在我的心上，
像朝陽的沉默灑落在已收割的孤寂田野上。

318

I long for the Island of Songs
across this heaving Sea of Shouts.

我渴望跨越這波濤洶湧的嚎叫之海，
抵達歌聲之島。

319

The prelude of the night is commenced in the music of the sunset, in its solemn hymn to the ineffable dark.

夜的序曲始於落日樂章，
那是對難以言喻的黑暗所譜的莊嚴讚歌。

320

I have scaled the peak and found no shelter in fame's bleak and barren height. Lead me, my Guide, before the light fades, into the valley of quiet where life's harvest mellows into golden wisdom.

我攀上高峰，發現名聲所在的高處，荒蕪貧瘠，無處躲藏。
我的嚮導，請引導我在光明漸逝前，進入沉靜的山谷吧，
在那裡，生命的收穫會熟成為金黃的智慧。

321

Things look phantastic in this dimness of the dusk—the spires whose bases are lost in the dark and tree tops like blots of ink. I shall wait for the morning and wake up to see thy city in the light.

在暮色朦朧裡，事物顯得奇幻
—尖塔底層沒入黑暗，樹頂如墨點斑斑。
我將等待黎明，甦醒時，就會看到城市沐浴在光明裡。

322

I have suffered and despaired and known death
and I am glad that I am in this great world.

我曾受苦絕望，亦曾體會過死亡，
我很慶幸自己能活在這個偉大世界。

323

There are tracts in my life that are bare and silent.
They are the open spaces
where my busy days had their light and air.

我的生命中，存著荒蕪寂寥之地。
如一處曠野，
讓我在奔忙之日得以擁有日光與空氣。

324

Release me from my unfulfilled past clinging to me from
behind making death difficult.

我那尚未圓滿的過去，從身後纏繞著我，使我難以死去，
請從那裡將我釋放吧。

325

Let this be my last word, that I trust in thy love.

「我相信你的愛。」請讓這句話做為我的遺言。

　　羅賓德拉納德・泰戈爾（Rabindranath Tagore, 1861-1941）是一位享譽世界的印度詩人、小說家、藝術家、思想家與社會活動家，是第一位獲得諾貝爾文學獎的亞洲人，一生寫了 50 多部詩集，被稱為「詩聖」。

　　他出生在印度一個富有哲學與文學修養的貴族家庭，8 歲就開始寫詩，13 歲便能對長詩與頌歌體詩集進行創作，展現出其非凡的文學天賦。1913 年他因自譯的英文版《吉檀迦利》榮獲諾貝爾文學獎，自此躋身於世界文壇。

　　他的作品具有極高的歷史、藝術價值，深受民眾喜愛。其主要詩作有不少被世人廣知，如《新月集》、《吉檀迦利》、《漂鳥集》、《採果集》、《園丁集》等。除了諸多詩集外，還創作了 12 部中長篇小說，100 多部短篇小說，20 多部劇本以及大量的文學、哲學、政治論著，並在 70 歲時開始學習繪畫，此外還創作了數量繁多的各類歌曲，影響後世甚鉅。

　　《漂鳥集》是泰戈爾於 1913 年所創作的代表作之一，也是世界最傑出詩集中的一部佳作。該詩集共收短詩 325 首，是一部富於哲理的英文格言詩集。

　　該詩集中包含了兩種背景，其中一部分是由泰戈爾自譯，以孟加拉文格言著寫的詩集《碎玉集》，另一部分則是在他 1916 年訪問日本的三個月間即興創作的英文詩作。所以這一詩集有著鮮明的深刻哲理與篇幅簡潔的特色。

「在暮色朦朧裡，事物顯得奇幻

　一尖塔底層沒入黑暗，樹頂如墨點斑斑。

　我將等待黎明，甦醒時，就會看到城市沐浴在光明裡。」

　　日出與日落、背叛與自由、火花與冰刃、夏花與秋葉這些矛盾的存在，都被泰戈爾以凝練的語句融合成深刻的人生哲理，成為引領世人尋求智慧與探求真理的源泉。

　　這一部乍看僅由零碎的思緒所組成的散文詩集，卻抒發著對人生、自然的諸多省思。泰戈爾以抒情的詩篇記錄著他對人生、自然與宇宙的深刻體悟，藉助詩篇給予世人許多人生啟示。初讀這些小詩，清新之感，猶如初雪降落後的清晨，看著窗外閃亮著冰晶的積雪，韻味獨到、引人深思。

關於譯者

　　鄭振鐸（1898-1958），著名文學家、作家、翻譯家和文物考古學家，同時也是新文化和新文學運動的宣導者。

　　他在 1922 年和 1923 年兩年間翻譯出版了泰戈爾的《漂鳥集》與《新月集》，從此便開始系統、大量地對泰戈爾的詩歌進行翻譯。這些譯作對當時的文壇產生了重要影響，亦促進中國新文學與西洋文學的交流。

　　因鄭振鐸主要翻譯的是泰戈爾的詩歌及印度古代的寓言，在他逝世後，印度的著名學者海曼歌・比斯瓦斯在 1958 年《悼念鄭振鐸》一文中寫道：「他可能是第一個把印度古典文學和現代文學介紹給中國讀者的人，他同樣是當前中印文化交流的先驅。」海曼歌・比斯瓦斯對鄭振鐸在印度文化方面的翻譯貢獻給予極高的評價。

1861	0	5月7日，羅賓德拉納特·泰戈爾出生於孟加拉加爾各答市的喬拉桑格，為家中十四子。
1869	8	開始練習寫詩。
1874	13	被錄取至聖澤維爾學校。
1875	14	母親去世。在《甘露市場報》上發表愛國詩篇；發表長篇敘事詩《野花》。離開聖澤維爾學校。
1877	16	發表第一篇短篇小說《女乞丐》以及敘事詩《詩人的故事》
1878	17	赴英國留學。於《婆羅蒂》雜誌上連載《旅歐書札》。
1880	19	從英國返回印度。
1881	20	發表音樂劇《蟻垤仙人的天才》。1882年出版《暮歌集》。於《婆羅蒂》連載長篇歷史小說《皇后市場》。發表詩劇《破碎的心》。雜文集《雜論》出版。
1882	21	開始創作《晨歌集》並於1883年出版。
1883	22	與穆里納莉妮·黛維結婚。
1884	23	擔任「梵社」秘書。發表歌劇《大自然的報復》。發表詩集《畫與歌集》、《帕努辛赫詩抄》。發表短篇小說《河邊的台階》。
1885	24	創作長篇歷史小說《賢哲王》。12月，國大黨

成立。

1886	25	長女瑪圖莉萊達出生，詩集《剛與柔》出版。
1888	27	長子羅提德拉納特出生。
1889	28	寫出無韻詩體劇本《國王和皇后》
1890	29	離開孟買，前往義大利、英國和法國旅行。次女蕾努卡出生。詩集《心靈集》出版。將《賢哲王》改編成詩劇，題名為《犧牲》上演。
1891	30	開始持續創作《郵政局長》、《還債》…等短篇小說。與侄子蘇倫創辦文學月刊《實踐》，直到 1895 年停刊。發表遊記《旅歐日記》。
1892	31	發表詩劇《齊德拉》，並於 1936 年改編成舞劇。短篇小說《摩訶摩耶》，《喀布爾人》發表。
1893	32	短篇小說《棄絕》和《素芭》等發表。
1894	33	小兒子索明德拉納特出生。擔任孟加拉文學協會副主席。出版短篇小說集《小說匯編》一、二集、《太陽和烏雲》。詩集《金色船集》出版。發表詩劇《離別時的詛咒》。
1895	34	創作短篇小說《飢餓的石頭》，與侄子蘇倫德羅納特合創黃麻經營企業。
1896	35	詩集《江河集》、《繽紛集》、《收穫集》出版。創作詩劇《瑪麗妮》。
1898	37	主編《婆羅蒂》雜誌。英國政府通過「反煽動法」，在加爾各答群眾集會上發表名為《窒息》的演說，嚴厲譴責英國殖民當局對民族主義運

		動領袖提拉克的迫害。
1899	38	加爾各答流行鼠疫，協助救治患者。侄子波朗德拉納特去世。創辦的企業倒閉。發表短詩集《塵埃集》。
1900	39	出版詩集《故事詩集》、《故事集》、《剎那集》和《幻想集》。
1901	40	在聖蒂尼克坦成立梵學書院。任《孟加拉觀察》雜誌編輯，直至 1906 年止。於該雜誌連載長篇小說《眼中沙》。詩集《祭品集》出版。
1902	41	辦學因經濟困難，典賣土地和妻子的首飾。11月 23 日妻子病逝，寫哀悼詩，1903 年結集出版，題為《懷念集》。
1903	42	二女蕾努卡病逝。出版詩集《兒童集》。於《孟加拉觀察》連載長篇小說《沈船》。
1905	44	1 月 15 日，父親於加爾各答逝世。創辦政治性月刊《寶庫》。積極參與反對殖民主義愛國運動。創作現為孟加拉國國歌的《金色的孟加拉》等大量愛國歌曲。
1906	45	送長子羅提德拉納特到美國學習農業科學。出版《沈船》單行本，發表詩集《渡口集》。
1907	46	於《外鄉人》上連載長篇小說《戈拉》。回聖蒂尼克坦從事文學創作與教育活動。發表論文《疾病與治療》。出版散文集《五彩繽紛》和《膜拜品德》，論文集《古代文學》、《民間文學》、《文學》、《現代文學》，劇本《滑稽劇本集》，

		雜文集《幽默》。小兒子去世。
1908	47	主持孟加拉邦政治協商會議。發表論文集《國王和人民》、《集體》、《社會》、《教育》和《自治》。發表詩集《故事和敘事集》、《致敬集》。出版詩劇《秋天的節日》和散文劇《皇冠》。
1909	48	長子羅提德拉納特離美回國。發表劇本《懺悔》。出版宗教、哲學演講集《聖蒂尼克坦》1-8集。
1910	49	孟加拉語詩集《吉檀迦利》出版。長篇小說《戈拉》出版。散文劇本《暗室之王》發表。於《外鄉人》上連載《回憶錄》，1912年出版單行本。編寫劇本《郵局》，1912年發表。創作歌曲《人民的意志》，1950年1月24日成為印度國歌。演講集《聖蒂尼克坦》12-13集出版。
1912	51	孟加拉文學協會為他舉辦慶祝會。5月27日，動身前往英、美國，直至第二年9月4日返回印度。詩集《吉檀迦利》英譯版出版。
1913	52	英文詩集《吉檀迦利》出版獲得諾貝爾文學獎。加爾各答大學授予名譽文學博士學位。英文詩集《園丁集》、《漂鳥集》、《新月集》出版。
1914	53	發表短篇小說《一個女人的信》。
1915	54	甘地訪問聖蒂尼克坦，泰戈爾會見甘地。獲英皇授予爵士榮銜。演講集《聖蒂尼克坦》14集出版，第二年出版15-17集。

1916	55	到訪日本和美國分別發表題為《國家主義》、《人格》等演說。長篇小說《家庭與世界》和《四個人》出版。發表詩集《鴻雁》與英文詩集《採果集》和《漂鳥集》。劇本《春之循環》和短篇小集《小說七篇》出版。
1917	56	於加爾各答的印度國大黨會議上宣讀詩篇《印度的祈禱》。
1918	57	大女兒去世。詩集《遁逃集》出版。
1919	58	憤怒抗議英國殖民當局在阿姆利則槍殺無辜群眾，宣佈放棄英國政府授予爵士稱號。發表遊記《訪日散記》。
1920	59	前往英國、法國、荷蘭和美國。為國際大學募捐。短篇小說集《第二個》出版。
1921	60	3月回國歸途中經英國又到法國，之後訪問德國、丹麥、瑞典、奧地利等國。於巴黎會見羅曼·羅蘭。在德國會見托馬斯·曼。7月回印度。12月23日國際大學正式成立，將聖蒂尼克坦的財產捐給國際大學。劇本《還債》出版。英譯本《沈船》、英文本《游思集》出版。
1922	61	訪問南印度和錫蘭（今斯里蘭卡），在可倫坡和加勒舉行了一系列講座。12月長兄去世。創作散文詩集《隨想集》。發表象徵劇《摩克多塔拉》。出版兒童詩集《童年的濕婆集》。
1923	62	將已發表著作的版權交付國際大學。《國際大學》季刊、英文版《戈拉》出版。參與劇目《犧

牲》的演出。發表音樂劇《春天》。

1924	63	於加爾各答大學發表文學主題演講。訪問中國，在上海、濟南、北京等地發表演說，會見梅蘭芳等知名藝文界人士，並與末代皇帝溥儀會面。訪問日本後回國。應邀訪問秘魯。創作《西行日記》和詩作《普爾比集》。
1925	64	1月離開布宜諾斯艾利斯前往義大利等地。2月回國。5月泰戈爾於聖蒂尼克坦會見甘地，但對不合作運動有著不同看法。年底，被選為印度哲學大會主席。
1926	65	於達卡大學發表演說。再次應邀出國，訪問義大利、英國、挪威、奧地利、瑞典、丹麥、德國、捷克、南斯拉夫、羅馬尼亞、匈牙利、保加利亞、希臘再經埃及回國。出版詩作《隨感集》；發表劇本《舞女的膜拜》、《獨身者協會》、《南迪妮》、《報復心理》、《最後一場雨》。
1927	66	著手創作長篇小說《糾纏》。在巴拉特普爾主持印地文學會議。發表劇本《舞王》。訪問馬來西亞、印尼和泰國。於《千姿百態》雜誌上連載《爪哇通訊》。
1928	67	與印度著名政治活動家、哲學家奧羅賓多會面。訪問錫蘭（今斯里蘭卡）和班加羅爾。發表劇本《最後的拯救》。創作長篇小說《最後的詩篇》。
1929	68	訪問加拿大、日本和南西貢。發表詩集書信集

《旅行者》。

1930	69	出訪法國、英國、德國、瑞士、俄國、美國，並於上述的一些國家舉辦畫展。在英國牛津大學發表主題為《人的宗教》的演講。開始在《僑民》雜誌發表《俄國書簡》，1931年集結出版。
1931	70	在印度市政大廳隆重慶祝70大壽。發表劇本《新穎》和《擺脫詛咒》。出版詩集《聚寶集》，《森林之聲集》和《通俗讀物集》。《泰戈爾全集》出版。
1932	71	抗議英國殖民當局逮捕甘地。出訪伊朗和伊拉克。唯一的孫子去世。出版詩集《再次集》和《總結集》，劇本《時間的流逝》發表。英文詩集《金色之書》出版。
1933	72	於加爾各答發表印度啟蒙主義先驅羅姆·摩罕的演說，在安得拉大學以《人》為題發表演講。詩集《五彩集》發表。劇本《紙牌王國》、《不可接觸的姑娘》和《竹笛》發表。中篇小說《兩姐妹》發表。
1934	73	率領國際大學業餘舞劇團前往錫蘭（今斯里蘭卡）和南印度巡迴演出。
1935	74	走訪北印度，並在幾所大學發表演說，為國際大學募籌資金。發表詩集《最後的星期集》和《小徑集》。英文論文集《東方和西方》出版。《泰戈爾歌曲二十六首》出版。
1936	75	在加爾各答針對教育問題發表演講。英文論文

集《使教育符合國情》發表。詩集《葉盤集》和《黑牛集》出版。遊記《瀛洲遊記》出版。論文集《文學的道路》和《韻律》出版。

1937	76	在加爾各答大學以孟加拉語發表演說。在聖蒂尼克坦主持國際大學中國學院成立典禮。著文《印度和中國》。出版詩集《非洲集》、《錯位集》和《兒歌之畫集》。短篇小說集《他》出版。
1938	77	寫信給日本詩人野口米次郎，譴責日本帝國主義侵略中國的罪行。詩集《晚祭集》和《邊緣集》出版。
1939	78	詩集《戲謔集》、《天燈集》出版。發表舞劇《解放》和《薩瑪》。
1940	79	泰戈爾在聖蒂尼克坦最後一次會見甘地。牛津大學授予泰戈爾博士學位。病情轉劇，被送往加爾各答就醫。英文自傳《我的童年》出版。詩集《新生集》、《嗩吶集》、《病榻集》出版。短篇小說集《三個同伴》出版。
1941	80	4月發表公開演說，題為《文明的危機》。7月病情惡化在加爾各答動手術。8月7日在加爾各答祖居與世長辭。詩集《康復集》、《生辰集》、《兒歌集》和《最後的作品集》等出版。

Memo

泰戈爾詩選漂鳥集 /泰戈爾著；鄭振鐸譯；
-- 三版. -- 臺北市：笛藤, 2022.03
　　面；　公分
中英對照雙語有聲版
ISBN 978-957-710-849-4（平裝）

867.51　　　　　　　　111002988

2022年3月25日　三版第一刷　定價300元

著　　　者	泰戈爾
譯　　　者	鄭振鐸
審　　　譯	陳珮馨
編　　　輯	江品萱
美術編輯	王舒玕
總　編　輯	洪季楨
編輯企劃	笛藤出版
發　行　所	八方出版股份有限公司
發　行　人	林建仲
地　　　址	台北市中山區長安東路二段171號3樓3室
電　　　話	(02) 2777-3682
傳　　　真	(02) 2777-3672
總　經　銷	聯合發行股份有限公司
地　　　址	新北市新店區寶橋路235巷6弄6號2樓
電　　　話	(02)2917-8022 · (02)2917-8042
製　版　廠	造極彩色印刷製版股份有限公司
地　　　址	新北市中和區中山路二段380巷7號1樓
電　　　話	(02)2240-0333 · (02)2248-3904
郵撥帳戶	八方出版股份有限公司
郵撥帳號	19809050

漂鳥集

泰戈爾詩選／

泰戈爾詩選

附
情境配樂
中英朗讀QR Code
百紀念珍藏套票

Stray Birds